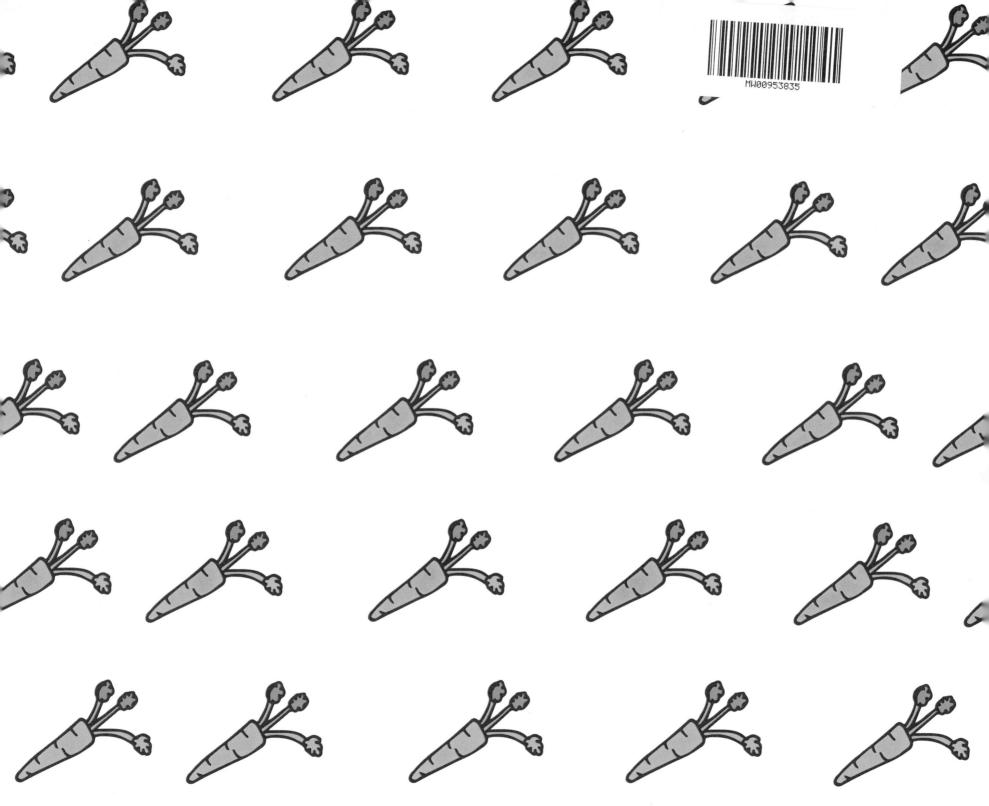

For Caleb & Pico . . .

Written by Jeff Coffin
Illustrated by Augie Haas
Edited by Jennifer Rees
ISBN 978-1-953622-00-6
© 2020 Jeff Coffin & Augie Haas
www.jeffcoffin.com - www.augiehaas.com
Thanks to all the people out there reading to their kids.

The Rabbit, the Carrot, the Crow, and the Quarry

Written by: Jeff Coffin

Illustrated by: Augie Haas

"I can't fall asleep, Mommy," said the young bunny to his mother.
"I can't either," said the bunny's younger brother.
"Well, if you'll both close your eyes,
I'll give you a lovely surprise.
Here's a story-it's not about you, but another..."

A long time ago, in a time far from today,
There lived a young bunny who wore a beret.
His first name was Davey,
His fur was quite wavy,
And he loved to go outside and play.

His all-time favorite playtime
was to hop and to run,

And he loved to eat carrots,
he relished them, each one.

This day, as he hopped
and he bopped,

His carrot, he suddenly
dropped

Into a hole that was as big as
the sun.

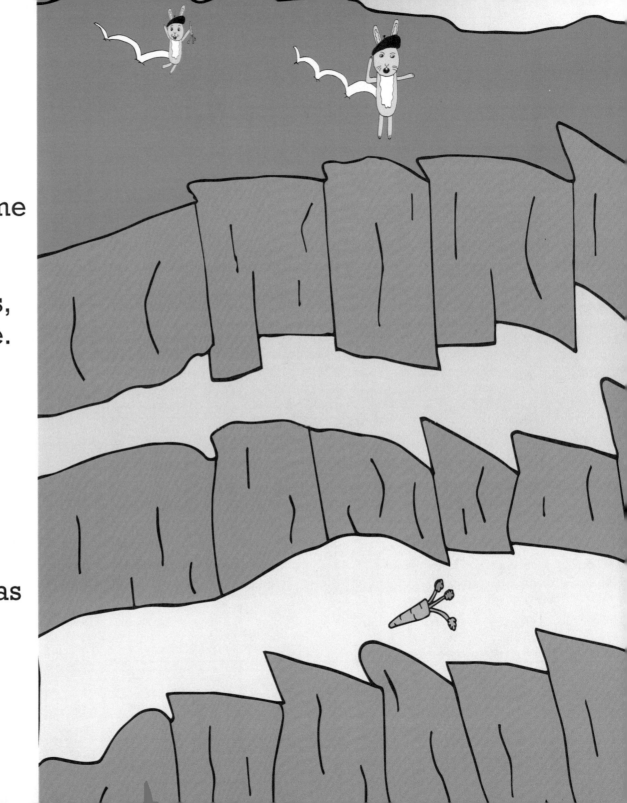

"Whatever will I do, I'm so hungry!" he cried.

He hopped to the great quarry and peered inside.

A big black crow from far, far below shrieked his best crow 'Hello'.

Then, to the bunny's side he did glide.

"Please, do me a favor, Crow," the bunny did plea.
"I'll promise you anything, if you'll do this for me..
Fetch the jewel I've dropped there.
It happened as I hopped," said the hare.
"And forever in your debt I will certainly be."

Well now, the crow saw it all happen, this is so very true,
Because that's what crows are known for knowing how to do.
In reality, the bunny's bad grip
Was what caused the slip.
Fresh with this knowing, down to the carrot the crow flew.

"If this is the jewel you desire, my friend,
    What lengths will you go to, and will you not bend?
    To get this fine piece,
    Your efforts can't cease!
    Now, your full attention to me you must lend."

"You cried you are hungry, I'll admit, so am I,
But you said it's a jewel, and that's a big lie.
It's crunchy and sweet,
A delicious, orange treat.
Tell the truth or I'll fly away with it, goodbye!"

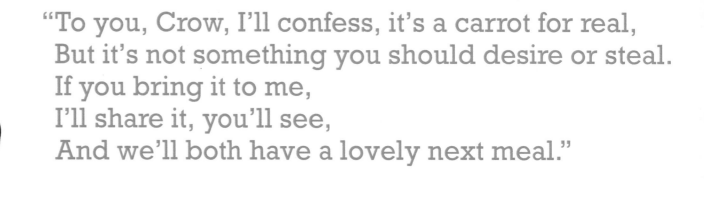

"To you, Crow, I'll confess, it's a carrot for real,
But it's not something you should desire or steal.
If you bring it to me,
I'll share it, you'll see,
And we'll both have a lovely next meal."

"Thank you, Bunny, for being truthful, honest, and kind
These are three things that no one should mind.
Let's share this nice food,
To decline would be rude!
And we both will feel satisfied, that you will find."

With that being said, the crow twice loudly crowed,
Then picked up and carried the once-fallen load.
To the rim he did fly,
Toward the brilliant blue sky...
To the bunny, his "jewel" he bestowed.

The bunny, now wiser, was feeling so glad.
For lunch, the carrot was what they both had.
He had made a new friend
On whom he could depend,
And friendships like that can never be bad.

Davey made his way back to his underground home.
It's called a "warren" and it's a big, open underground dome.
He shared his day's story
About the carrot, the crow, and the quarry.
He hoped that tomorrow again he could roam.

Suddenly his eyes, and his head too, felt so very tired,
And sleep was all that his full heart desired.
He laid down his head
On his very soft bed,
And thought of the crow,
whom he deeply admired.

Sleep. It came quickly and washed over his night.
He dreamed and he dreamed that he was in flight
With his new friend the crow
He had just started to know,
And dreamt about flying until nearly first light.

Mama bunny said softly that her story was through,
But tomorrow might bring another story she knew.

Now you won't hear a peep,
Everyone is done counting sheep.

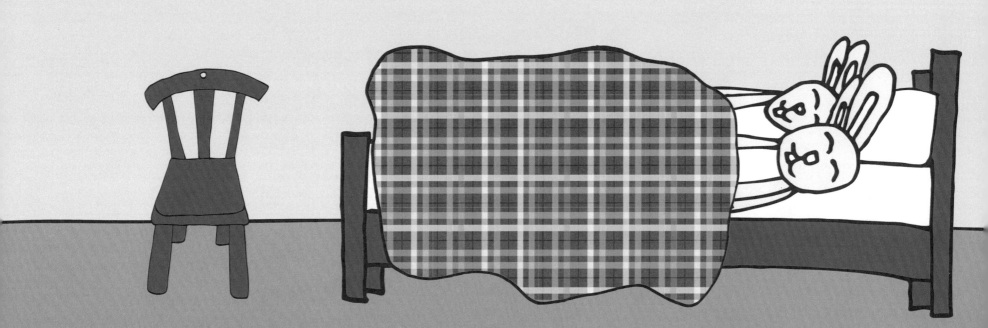

And they are all

fast asleep...

Just . . .

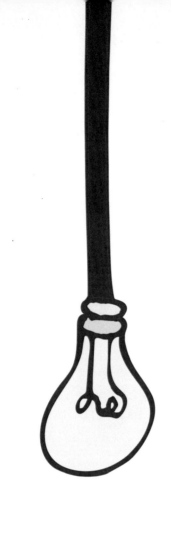

Like . . .

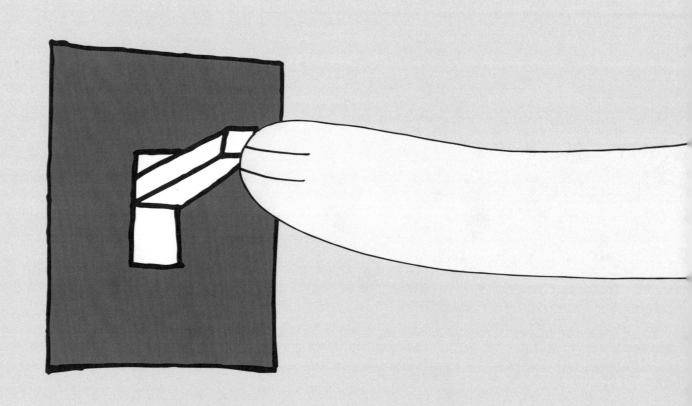

You.

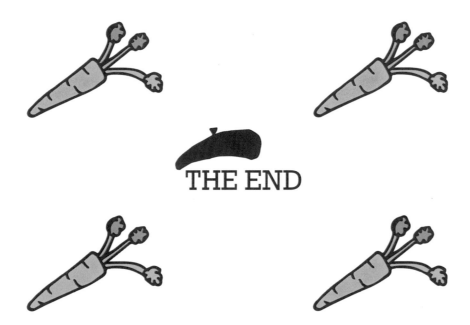

THE END

CPSIA information can be obtained
at www.ICGtesting.com
Printed in the USA
LVRC091029201021
700927LV00003B/106